WALT DISNEY'S Bambi

Friends of the Forest

A GOLDEN BOOK • NEW YORK

Western Publishing Company, Inc.,
Racine, Wisconsin 53404

ij

"Wake up, everyone!" chirped the bluebird one fine autumn morning. "The Prince is here!"

Bambi's friends watched as the handsome fawn walked gracefully down the path. The opossums called out their upside-down greetings, and the squirrel and chipmunk chattered hello, too.

"Today Bambi is going to the lake for the very first time," Thumper the bunny explained to the old owl. Then he added proudly, "And *I* will introduce him to the animals who live there."

The owl looked down at Bambi and said, "Remember what your mother told you, young fellow. Be very alert in the forest, and run away quickly if ever you meet with danger."

Bambi listened carefully, for surely his mother—and the wise old owl—knew what was best for him.

Not far away, Thumper's sisters had discovered a
small hollow log.

"Would you like to play, too, Bambi?" they asked
as they raced in one end and out the other.

"Oh, I'd like to, but I'm too big for *that* game,"
Bambi replied politely. "Besides, I am very busy."

Then Bambi and Thumper came to the burrow where their friend Flower lived. They asked the little skunk if he wanted to join them, but Flower said no.

"There's a very mean fox in the woods," he warned, peeking out from behind two big daisies.

Now, Thumper knew that *he* should be afraid, too.
But he had so many things to do today that he just
didn't have time to worry about a fox.

So off he hopped, and Bambi followed close behind
as Thumper led the way deeper and deeper into the
big forest.

"Bambi is becoming very brave," said Mother Quail as the fawn pranced by, and her family agreed. Bambi had never before been so far from home, and never *ever* before had he been away from his mother.

When they finally arrived at the lake, Bambi turned to Thumper. "It *is* as beautiful as you said it would be," he said. And then, sounding a bit disappointed, he asked, "But where are all the animals?"

Out of the tall grass came a big, green frog. "They're here, all right," he told them, "but they're hiding. That wicked fox was here this morning."

And then, with a hop and a *plop,* he disappeared into the water.

The animals *were* there, and they soon came out, one by one, to meet the handsome Prince.

Mother Duck was the first to appear. She called to her ducklings, telling them to come out, too.

Bambi was delighted! He had never before seen birds who could swim. Nor, for that matter, had he seen birds who could do such special tricks!

Bambi stepped back, surprised, as the next animal
—a prickly-looking fellow—came waddling out from
behind a big rock.

Thumper chuckled. "Don't worry, Bambi," he said.
"This is a porcupine. See? He wants to be your friend."

Next, Bambi met Bernice. He admired her fine, fluffy coat, and then, very curious, he asked, "Why does she wear a mask?"

Thumper chuckled again. "That's not a mask, Bambi! That's the way a raccoon is *supposed* to look!"

Although the beavers were busy working, they, too, came over to meet Bambi.

"I've seen your father," the youngest beaver told Bambi. "He comes here often to take a drink."

Bambi was just taking a cool, refreshing drink him-self, when suddenly he heard a chipmunk's loud, nervous chatter. "*Chi-ch-ch-ch-ch-ch-chi!* Run and hide! The fox is near!"

With a hurry and a scurry, the animals quickly
rushed away. But little Thumper, who was so far from
his safe, snug home, **didn't** dare to move. *Maybe the
fox won't notice me,* he **thought.**

Bambi was frightened, too, but he knew that his friend was in worse danger than he was. He saw the large fox slowly and slyly creeping toward the tiny, helpless bunny.

Bambi thought quickly. *Surely I can outrun that fox!*

So, without a bit of hesitation, Bambi leaped between the fox and Thumper, and, just as Bambi had planned, the fox *did* start to chase him!

Through the forest they ran, over logs and bushes and rocks and twigs, with the fox never far behind. Bambi's hooves pounded the ground, and his heart beat fast as the fox got closer and closer.

And then, at the very moment when Bambi felt he could run no more, a large, powerful stag stepped out from behind a tree.

He lowered his majestic antlers and charged. The fox—who was frightened indeed—stopped in his tracks, turned hastily, and dashed off into the woods.

Breathless, Bambi looked up at the stag. He knew
that this must be his father, the mighty King of the
Forest, whom his mother had told him so much about.

The King spoke to his little son. "You didn't know it, Bambi, but you are much too young to outrun such a fox," he said in a deep, kindly voice. "But I am very proud of you. The bluebird has told me how you helped your friend."

That same bluebird also told everyone *else* what had
happened, and by the time the animals arrived at the
hill, they saw a very happy Bambi—safe and sound—
standing proudly beside his father.

Thumper, who was the happiest of them all, hopped over to Bambi and looked gratefully up at his friend. "Thank you for saving my life, Bambi," he said. "You're not only my *best* friend, but you're my *bravest* friend, too!"